jE   Yee
      Roses sing on new
snow.

DATE DUE

6-15-95	icc		

Roses Sing on New Snow

Text copyright © 1991 by Paul Yee
Illustrations copyright © 1991 by Harvey Chan

Macmillan Publishing Company is part of the
Maxwell Communication Group of Companies.

Macmillan Publishing Company
866 Third Avenue
New York, NY 10022

Originally published by Groundwood Books,
Toronto, Canada.

First American edition
Printed in Hong Kong

1 3 5 7 9 10 8 6 4 2

Library of Congress Cataloging-in-Publication Data is available.
ISBN 0-02-793622-8

Roses Sing on New Snow

A Delicious Tale

BY PAUL YEE

ILLUSTRATED BY HARVEY CHAN

Macmillan Publishing Company   *New York*

Maxwell Macmillan International
New York Oxford Singapore Sydney

SEVEN days a week, every week of the year, Maylin cooked in her father's restaurant. It was a spot well known throughout the New World for its fine food.

But when compliments and tips were sent to the chef, they never reached Maylin because her father kept the kitchen door closed and told everyone that it was his two sons who did all the cooking.

Maylin's father and brothers were fat and lazy from overeating, for they loved food.

Maylin loved food too, but for different reasons. To Chinatown came men lonely and cold and bone-tired. Their families and wives waited in China.

But a well-cooked meal would always make them smile.
So Maylin worked to renew their spirits and used only the
best ingredients in her cooking.

Then one day it was announced that the governor of South China was coming to town. For a special banquet, each restaurant in Chinatown was invited to bring its best dish.

Maylin's father ordered her to spare no expense and to use all her imagination on a new dish. She shopped in the market for fresh fish and knelt in her garden for herbs and greens.

In no time she had fashioned a dish of delectable flavors and aromas, which she named Roses Sing on New Snow.

Maylin's father sniffed happily and went off to the banquet, dressed in his best clothes and followed by his two sons.

Now the governor also loved to eat. His eyes lit up like lanterns at the array of platters that arrived. Every kind of meat, every color of vegetable, every bouquet of spices was present. His chopsticks dipped eagerly into every dish.

When he was done, he pointed to Maylin's bowl and said, "That one wins my warmest praise! It reminded me of China, and yet it transported me far beyond. Tell me, who cooked it?"

Maylin's father waddled forward and repeated the lie he had told so often before. "Your Highness, it was my two sons who prepared it."

"Is that so?" The governor stroked his beard thoughtfully. "Then show my cook how the dish is done. I will present it to my emperor in China and reward you well!"

Maylin's father and brothers rushed home. They burst into the kitchen and forced Maylin to list all her ingredients. Then they made her demonstrate how she had chopped the fish and carved the vegetables and blended the spices.

They piled everything into huge baskets and then hurried back.

A stove was set up before the governor and his cook. Maylin's brothers cut the fish and cleaned the vegetables and ground the spices. They stoked a fire and cooked the food. But with one taste, the governor threw down his chopsticks.

"You imposters! Do you take me for a fool?" he bellowed. "That is not Roses Sing on New Snow!"

Maylin's father tiptoed up and peeked. "Why . . . why, there is one spice not here," he stuttered.

"Name it and I will send for it!" roared the impatient governor.

But Maylin's father had no reply, for he knew nothing about spices.

Maylin's older brother took a quick taste and said, "Why, there's one vegetable missing!"

"Name it, and my men will fetch it!" ordered the governor.

But no reply came, for Maylin's older brother knew nothing about food.

Maylin's other brother blamed the fishmonger. "He gave us the wrong kind of fish!" he cried.

"Then name the right one, and my men will fetch it!" said the governor.

Again there was no answer.

Maylin's father and brothers quaked with fear and fell to their knees. When the governor pounded his fist on the chair, the truth quickly spilled out. The guests were astounded to hear that a woman had cooked this dish. Maylin's father hung his head in shame as the governor sent for the real cook.

Maylin strode in and faced the governor and his men. "Your Excellency, you cannot take this dish to China!" she announced.

"What?" cried the governor. "You dare refuse the emperor a chance to taste this wonderful creation?"

"This is a dish of the New World," Maylin said. "You cannot recreate it in the Old."

But the
governor
ignored her
words and
scowled. "I can
make your
father's life
miserable here,"
he threatened her.
So she said, "Let you
and I cook side by
side, so you can see for
yourself."

The guests gasped at her daring request. However, the governor nodded, rolled up his sleeves, and donned an apron. Together, Maylin and the governor cut and chopped. Side by side they heated two woks, and then stirred in identical ingredients.

When the two dishes were finally finished, the governor took a taste from both. His face paled, for they were different.

"What is your secret?" he demanded. "We selected the same ingredients and cooked side by side!"

"If you and I sat down with paper and brush and black ink, could we bring forth identical paintings?" asked Maylin.

From that day on Maylin was renowned in Chinatown as a great cook and a wise person. Her fame even reached as far as China.

But the emperor, despite the governor's best efforts, was never able to taste that most delicious New World dish, nor to hear Roses Sing on New Snow.